BLAM! The stack of books crashed to the floor right behind the desk where the dark-haired girl was sitting. She did not move or blink an eye at the sound of the crash.

The boys looked at one another and shrugged their shoulders. "Hey, I bet this'll make her jump," Eddie Thompson bragged to his classmates. Sticking two fingers in his mouth, Eddie blew a high-pitched whistle. SCREECH!

Again, the dark-haired girl did not move. She quietly flipped her long hair over one shoulder and continued reading the book in front of her.

ALEX

Crocodile Meatloaf

Nancy Simpson Levene

Chariot VICTOR
PUBLISHING
A DIVISION OF COOK COMMUNICATIONS

It is he who saved us and chose us for his holy work,
not because we deserved it but because that was his plan
long before the world began—to show his love and
kindness to us through Christ.
II Timothy 1:9
The Living Bible

Chariot Books is an imprint of Chariot Victor Publishing,

a division of Cook Communications, Colorado Springs, Colorado 80918

Cook Communications, Paris, Ontario

Kingsway Communications, Eastbourne, England

CROCODILE MEATLOAF
© 1993 by Nancy R. Simpson for text and GraphCom
Corporation for interior illustrations.

Cover design by Bill Paetzold
Cover illustration by Neal Hughes

First Printing, 1993
Printed in the United States of America
98 97 96   7 6 5 4

Library of Congress Cataloging-in-Publication Data
Levene, Nancy S., 1949-
Crocodile meatloaf / by Nancy Simpson Levene.
        p.   cm.
Summary: As she becomes friends with Rachel, a deaf girl who has
joined her sixth-grade class, Alex begins to feel that God has given
her a mission to protect Rachel from the boy who is tormenting her.
ISBN 0-7814-0000-7
[1. Deaf—Fiction. 2. Physically handicapped—Fiction. 3.
Schools—Fiction. 4. Christian life—Fiction.] I. Title.
PZ7.L5724Cr 1993
[Fic]—dc 20

                                    92-32615
                                    CIP AC

CONTENTS

To the Father, the Son,
and the Spirit
who have guided my pen
and shared their glory with me;
and
To Julie Smith
who believed in Alex
from the first
and whose editing contributed
so much to the series.

ACKNOWLEDGMENTS

Thank you, Emily Northcraft, for helping to inspire this book and for being a wonderful friend and super softball player. Thank you, Cara, Mom and Dad, Patti and Lara Kupka, for your unfailing support through the entire Alex series. Thank you, Julie Smith and Sue Leaf for your expert editing. A big thank-you to the many Alex readers who have remained loyal to the series and have sent me such wonderful letters and pictures. Most importantly, thank You, Jesus, for choosing me to write the Alex series.

CHAPTER 1

A Broken Window and Police

BLAM! The stack of books crashed to the floor right behind the desk where the dark-haired girl was sitting. She did not move or blink an eye at the sound of the crash.

The boys looked at one another and shrugged their shoulders. "Hey, I bet this'll make her jump," Eddie Thompson bragged to his classmates. Sticking two fingers in his mouth, Eddie blew a high-pitched whistle. SCREECH!

Again, the dark-haired girl did not move. She quietly flipped her long hair over one shoulder and continued reading the book in front of her.

Alex sighed and rolled her eyes to the

ceiling. Eddie and his friends were tormenting Rachel again. Rachel was deaf. Her parents had recently enrolled her at Kingswood Elementary School for the last half of sixth grade. They wanted to see if she could get along in a regular classroom. Rachel was very smart and could read lips amazingly well. She would get along just fine if the boys would leave her alone. They were trying to see if they could make a noise loud enough for her to hear.

"Leave Rachel alone," Alex told Eddie.

"Try and make me," Eddie made a face at Alex.

Although Alex was tempted to teach Eddie a lesson in manners, something else caught her attention. Even though Rachel did not seem to be bothered by the boys behind her, Alex noticed a small tear escape from one of Rachel's eyes and roll down her cheek. She brushed it away quickly.

"So Rachel is bothered by the boys

teasing her," Alex told herself. But she had no more time to think about it. Her teacher, Mrs. Shivers, called for everyone's attention. It was time to begin the daily geography lesson.

After school, Alex and her friends, Janie, Julie, and Lorraine, walked outside and down the front sidewalk of the school. At the parking lot, they turned to go down to the softball field at the far edge of the playground. Today was the first day of spring softball practice.

As Alex walked across the parking lot, a familiar figure caught her eye. It was Rachel Kohlman, the deaf girl in her class. She stood in the parking lot looking sad and lonely.

Alex remembered how the boys had teased Rachel and how the tear had rolled down her cheek. Rachel seemed so alone, almost as if she didn't know how to fit in with the others. Was there something Alex could do to help Rachel?

Taking a deep breath, Alex decided to try. "Wait a minute," she told her friends. She ran over to Rachel.

"Hi, Rachel," Alex said brightly, coming up behind her. She then realized that Rachel could not possibly hear her, and unless she stood directly in front of her, would not even know that Alex was speaking.

Alex moved to stand in front of Rachel. "Hi, Rachel," she tried again, this time making sure that Rachel could read her lips.

"Hi," Rachel replied shyly and looked quickly at the ground. She seemed embarrassed whenever anyone spoke to her.

"Uh, Rachel," Alex tapped her on the arm to get her attention. "Would you like to come to softball practice with me? We are just starting the season. Maybe you'd like to be on the team?"

Immediately, Rachel's eyes lit up. She even smiled a tiny smile. "Okay," she agreed.

"Come on," Alex motioned for Rachel to walk with her and her friends.

When the girls reached the softball diamond, their coach, Mr. Glover, and several teammates were already on the field warming up.

As she approached her coach, Alex wondered what he would think of Rachel. Maybe she should have talked to her coach before inviting Rachel to join the team. Alex shrugged. It was too late to think about that now.

"Hi, Mr. Glover," Alex said as they neared the coach. "This is Rachel Kohlman. She wants to be on our team."

"Oh?" Mr. Glover looked surprised. "Hello, Rachel," he said and held out his hand.

Rachel shook hands shyly. "Hi," she responded and immediately looked at the ground.

"Have you ever played softball before, Rachel?" Mr. Glover asked.

Rachel did not answer. She was too

busy looking at the ground to read Mr. Glover's lips. She could not hear that he was speaking to her.

Alex decided she better take charge. She tapped Rachel's arm to get her attention. When Rachel looked up, Alex asked, "Have you ever played softball before, Rachel?"

"Yes," Rachel said and looked down at the ground again.

Alex tapped her arm a second time. "Where did you play softball?" she asked when Rachel looked up.

Rachel shrugged. "At home and school," she replied. She stared back down at the ground.

"Well, ask her what position she played," said Mr. Glover. Alex hoped he was not getting impatient. Her coach never did like to waste time at softball practice.

Alex tapped Rachel's arm again. "What position did you play?"

"Catcher," Rachel replied.

"CATCHER!" Alex and Mr. Glover shouted at once. The team desperately needed a catcher. Their regular one had moved out of town last season.

Mr. Glover began to smile. Then he began to whistle. Hurrying to the equipment bag, he yanked out the catcher's mask, helmet, chest protector, and shin guards. He began adjusting them to fit Rachel.

As soon as Rachel was outfitted in the catcher's gear, Mr. Glover motioned for her to take position behind home plate. He tossed a ball to Alex and told her to warm up on the mound. Alex was the team's pitcher.

Alex turned to go but then stopped and looked at her coach. "I, uh, forgot to tell you one thing about Rachel," she said.

"What's that?" Mr. Glover asked impatiently. He was in a hurry to get practice started.

"She's deaf," Alex replied and turned around to walk to the mound. She could feel her coach's eyes on her back all the way. When she turned to face him, he was staring at her, his mouth wide open in surprise.

Alex sighed. Had she been wrong to bring Rachel to practice? Could Rachel play softball without being able to hear? If it did not work out, it would all be Alex's fault.

Taking a deep breath, Alex took her position on the mound, wound up, and let a pitch sail through the air straight across the center of the plate. Rachel caught it with no problem.

"Strike!" her coach nodded with approval.

Alex threw another and another and another. Rachel caught the pitches perfectly, even digging some of the low ones out of the dirt.

When her coach called them in for batting practice, Alex could tell that he was pleased with Rachel's performance. He patted Rachel on the shoulder.

Looking her straight in the eye, he said, "Very good!"

Rachel smiled happily while Alex helped her take off the catcher's gear. They waited for their turns at bat.

Alex let Rachel bat first. Mr. Glover pitched. He made the mistake of throwing an easy-to-hit pitch right down the center of the plate. Rachel did not hesitate and socked the ball farther than Alex had seen any player hit it.

Everyone held their breath as the ball flew high into left field and over the fence that separated the school playground from the neighborhood houses. The ball hit the ground hard on the other side of the fence and bounced smack into a window in the side of a house. CRACK! SHATTER! The sound of breaking glass met their ears.

Mr. Glover stared at Rachel in disbelief. "I have never seen anyone hit the ball that hard!" he finally exclaimed.

Rachel was afraid that Mr. Glover

would be mad at her for breaking a
window. She stood with her hands
covering her mouth and had a horrified
look on her face.

Alex moved to Rachel's side. "It's
okay," she told her and then added,
"Great hit!" They watched as their coach
walked through left field to the fence. A
most unhappy-looking woman stood in
the yard of the house where the window
had been broken. She was holding a
softball.

As the girls waited for Mr. Glover to return, Alex suddenly noticed some unusual activity in the school parking lot. Something big was going on! A police car was parked there, and its lights were whirling. A policeman stood at its side talking to a small group of adults. Alex could see that Mrs. Larson, the school principal, was among the adults.

"Brussels sprouts, I wonder what's going on up there," Alex said half to herself and half to Rachel. Rachel, however, was not paying attention to Alex. She was anxiously watching the coach return from left field.

Mr. Glover was not upset in the least. In fact, he was in a jolly mood. When he reached Rachel, his face broke into a wide grin.

"Best hit I've seen in a long time!" he exclaimed. "Can't wait until the season starts!"

Rachel smiled back at Mr. Glover. So did Alex. Rachel was a good addition to the team. Despite the broken window, Alex was glad she had brought her to practice.

Practice began again. The girls batted and fielded. Alex worked up a sweat throwing pitch after pitch. She was just about ready to throw the last few pitches of the day, when out of the corner of her eye she glimpsed a uniformed figure striding onto the field. It was a police officer. Alex stopped her windup. Mr. Glover came out from behind home plate. He met the officer near the pitcher's mound. Alex was able to hear every word of their conversation.

"What can I do for you, Officer?" Mr. Glover asked.

"We have a report from the school of a missing child," the officer replied. "We were wondering if you noticed anything unusual. Have you seen any strange-looking people or cars hanging about?"

"No, can't say I have." Mr. Glover scratched his head under his ball cap.

"We've been busy with ball practice. Who is the missing child?"

"A twelve-year-old girl," the police officer answered.

Alex gasped. She knew every twelve year old in the school. "What is her name?" Alex asked the police officer.

He glanced at a small notebook he carried in his hand. "The child who is missing is named Rachel Kohlman."

CHAPTER 2

T-Bone Is Lost

Alex stared at the police officer in disbelief. Had he just said that Rachel Kohlman was missing? Alex glanced over her shoulder at Rachel. A very sick feeling in the pit of her stomach began to grow.

Mr. Glover also looked in Rachel's direction. Then he stared at Alex. "Uh, Officer, I think there's been some kind of mistake," the coach finally said. "You see, our catcher's name is Rachel Kohlman." Mr. Glover pointed at Rachel, who stood by the plate, the catcher's mask pushed back from her forehead. She frowned in confusion at all three of them.

The police officer looked surprised. "Rachel's mother has reported Rachel missing. She came to pick up her daughter after school and she was not there. We have been searching for Rachel for at least half an hour. Why is she here without her mother's knowledge?"

Mr. Glover threw up his hands. "I didn't know Rachel was here without her mother's knowledge. She came with Alex!" He pointed at Alex.

Alex swallowed hard and tried to smile as the police officer turned his stern gaze on her. "Uh, I just asked her to come with me to softball practice after school," Alex told him. "I didn't think about asking her mother."

"Rachel's mother is very worried about her," the officer replied. His face softened. "I know it might be difficult to communicate with Rachel because she cannot hear, but the next time you invite Rachel to go somewhere, make sure she has her mother's permission."

"Okay," Alex agreed.

She and Mr. Glover watched in amazement as the police officer began to speak to Rachel in sign language. Rachel made signs back to the officer. She handed Mr. Glover his softball mitt and catcher's mask and began to follow the police officer to the parking lot.

Alex grabbed her own mitt and hurried after Rachel and the police officer. She felt responsible for all the trouble and wanted to apologize to Rachel's mother.

As they neared the parking lot, a small, dark-haired woman ran toward them. The woman grabbed Rachel and hugged her. Then, taking Rachel by the shoulders and looking into her eyes, the woman asked, "Where have you been?"

Rachel acted extremely embarrassed. She shrugged and told her mother, "I've been at softball practice with Alex."

"I can see that," her mother looked amused. Rachel still wore the catcher's shin guards and chest protector. Her hair had fallen in her face, and her face was lined with grime and sweat from the catcher's mask. Her left side was filthy where she had slid in the dirt trying to make a play at home plate. She looked so comical that Mrs. Kohlman began to laugh. So did Alex and the police officer. Finally, Rachel joined them.

When all of the tension had passed, Mrs. Kohlman held out her hand to Alex. "Hello, you must be Alex," she said smiling. "I'm Irene Kohlman, Rachel's mother."

"Nice to meet you," Alex answered politely. "I'm Alex Brackenbury. I'm really sorry to have made you worry about Rachel. We're hoping that she can join our softball team. She's a great player."

"Why, that's nice of you, Alex," replied Mrs. Kohlman. "Do you want to join Alex's team, Rachel?"

Rachel nodded eagerly.

"Rachel has played all kinds of ball

games with her brothers and she played some at her previous school," Mrs. Kohlman said, "but she's never been on a real team before. Do you think she will do okay?"

"Oh, yeah," Alex assured Mrs. Kohlman. "She was great today! You can ask our coach. Here he comes now."

Mr. Glover walked toward them, lugging the equipment bag over his shoulder. He apologized to Rachel's mother for having Rachel at practice without her permission. He told her how well Rachel had done at practice, even telling her about the broken window. He assured her that his insurance would take care of it.

Rachel's mother gave Rachel permission to be on the softball team. Everyone was happy, but no one more than Rachel. Her face beamed with joy.

The next day, Alex asked Rachel to stay after school so they could practice pitching and catching. Now that she had a good catcher, Alex wanted to practice as much as she could. Because this was their last season in the elementary league, Alex was determined that her team would come out on top.

Rachel eagerly agreed. After making sure that Rachel's mother understood their plans, the girls headed across the playground to the ball diamond.

It was a beautiful spring day. The sun felt especially good as it shone warm on the girls' arms and faces. It brought the promise of summer with ball games and no school. Alex sighed happily. She opened her backpack and took out a ball and two gloves. She had brought an extra glove for Rachel.

The girls got into their positions, but Alex hadn't thrown more than five pitches when trouble arrived. Eddie Thompson and his group of friends appeared at the edge of the diamond. Eddie laughed out loud when he saw that it was Rachel catching Alex's pitches.

"You mean she plays ball?" Eddie asked, rudely stomping onto the field and pointing at Rachel. "You gotta be kidding!"

As Rachel read his lips, her face grew red in embarrassment.

"Yeah, nerd brain," Alex answered Eddie. "For your information, she's a dynamite catcher. She can also hit. Yesterday, she smacked one farther than I've ever seen anyone hit a ball, including you. She hit it over the fence and into one of those houses at the back of the playground!"

"Whew!" the other boys whistled. They were all impressed . . . all except Eddie.

"I don't believe it!" Eddie replied hotly.

"Just ask my coach," Alex retorted. "He's the one who had to pay for the window she broke!"

The other boys laughed. Eddie just scowled at Alex. "I won't believe it until I see it," he replied.

Alex shrugged and did her best to ignore the boys. They finally got tired of teasing and headed off toward the creek that ran at the back of the school. Alex breathed a sigh of relief to see them go.

Suddenly, a familiar noise reached her ears. Turning, Alex was surprised to see her own dog, T-Bone, running across the field toward her. The big black labrador barked excitedly. Behind him ran Alex's younger brother, Rudy, with an empty leash in his hand. Behind Rudy ran Jason, Rudy's best friend and next-door neighbor.

"Hi, Alex!" Rudy called as he ran. "We have come to play with you. Mom said you were here."

The boys stopped in front of Alex to catch their breath. "Whew! That dog can sure run!" they exclaimed.

"You know, you're not really supposed to let T-Bone off his leash," Alex told her ten-year-old brother.

"Yeah, I know," Rudy shrugged, "but I

figured it wouldn't matter on the playground. There's nobody here but you and Rachel and those boys over there." Rudy pointed at Eddie and his friends. They were now at the edge of the playground, heading for the creek.

"I guess it's okay," Alex nodded. T-Bone was frolicking in the grass not far from the diamond. "We'd better keep an eye on him though," Alex told Rudy.

The boys had brought a bat, so the four of them took turns pitching, batting, and playing the field. They had so much fun that they forgot all about keeping an eye on T-Bone. It wasn't until Alex happened to look up after pitching several fast balls to Rachel that she saw Eddie and his friends coaxing T-Bone through the gate in the fence that separated the playground from the creek bank.

"OH, NO!" she cried and dropped her mitt and the ball on the mound. She began running for the creek. "T-BONE! STOP! COME BACK HERE!" she hollered.

Rachel and the boys ran after her. Alex reached the creek ahead of them and charged after T-Bone, who was having a wonderful time exploring the creek. He ran this way and that way, galloping through the water and prancing up and down the muddy bank.

"T-BONE!" Alex called in desperation. The dog was getting farther and farther away from her. He could run much faster and was better at keeping his balance on the rocks and slippery bank.

"HA, HA!" Eddie and his friends laughed when Alex fell to her knees in the mud. "What's the matter, Alex? Having trouble walking in the creek?"

Alex burned with rage. She wanted to stop and punch Eddie. It was his fault that T-Bone was in the creek. But instead, Alex kept right after T-Bone. She did not want to lose the dog. Unfortunately, that is just what happened. The dog was too fast. He soon left them all behind and disappeared completely.

Alex, Rachel, Rudy, and Jason followed the creek for a long time. There was still no sign of T-Bone. Finally, they had to admit defeat and turned around to go back down the creek.

"He might have even left the creek and gone through the backyards into that neighborhood," Alex said, pointing to the houses that lined the creek bank.

"What should we do, Alex?" Rudy wailed. "It's all my fault. I shouldn't have let T-Bone off the leash."

"It's not all your fault," Alex tried to comfort her brother. "T-Bone would have been just fine if Eddie Thompson hadn't let him through the gate into the creek. I'd like to clobber that Eddie!"

Gritting her teeth, Alex started back down the creek with the others. They hadn't gone far when they met up with Eddie and his group of friends who had followed them in the search for T-Bone.

"Aw, what's the matter?" Eddie jeered at Alex. "Couldn't you find your doggy?"

That was too much for Alex. Anger burned inside her. She marched straight for Eddie, her fists clenched tightly. The other boys moved out of her way.

Before Eddie could react, Alex grabbed hold of him and jerked him down the bank. They both slipped in the mud, but Alex did not care. With a tremendous heave, Alex pushed Eddie into the water below!

"YEAHHHHOW!" Eddie hollered as he sprawled into the icy water. His friends hooted and hollered with laughter.

Alex did not wait for Eddie to get up. She motioned Rudy, Rachel, and Jason to hurry the rest of the way down the creek, through the gate, and back into the playground.

Just as they reached the playground, Rachel's mother drove into the parking lot. Alex said good-bye to Rachel, then she and the boys trudged back to the softball diamond. They gathered up the softball equipment and hurried home. After saying good-bye to Jason, Alex and Rudy burst through their front door, upsetting Father as he stood in the front hallway, a jacket in his hand.

"WHOA!" Father exclaimed and caught the door just before it slammed into his face. "I was just coming to look for you two," he told Alex and Rudy. "You are late coming home. Your mother was worried."

"T-Bone's lost!" Alex and Rudy told him.

"Lost?" Father looked surprised.

"What do you mean T-Bone is lost?" Mother asked, coming out of the kitchen.

"T-Bone's lost?" cried Barbara, their older sister. She ran down the stairs and into the front hallway.

Alex and Rudy poured out their story. When they had finished, they sank to the floor and could not stop the tears that flowed from their eyes.

"It's okay," Father reached down and hugged both children. "We'll find T-Bone. Let's go get the van and drive up and down the streets to look for him."

Alex, Rudy, and Barbara followed Father out the door and climbed into the new family minivan. Mother stayed home to answer the phone in case someone found T-Bone and called their phone number, which was printed on his dog tags.

Father and the children drove up and down every street in the neighborhood. They shouted T-Bone's name over and over. Father whistled. But still the dog did not come.

By now it was completely dark. Street-lights were on and so were lights in houses.

"I think we'd better go home," Father finally said.

"But what about T-Bone?" the children worried.

"We'll find him," Father assured them. "He has on his collar and dog tags with our name and phone number on them. Someone will find him and call us. Maybe somebody already has and Mother has the message at home."

They all brightened at that thought. But when they got home and rushed into the house to see if Mother had good news, she shook her head.

"No one has called about T-Bone," she said sadly. "I was hoping you had found him." There were tears in Mother's eyes. She loved T-Bone just as much as the children did.

"Now, now," Father tried to calm everyone. "Someone is bound to find him sooner or later, and when they do, they will call us."

"Can we say a prayer for T-Bone?" Alex asked.

"That's a good idea," Father agreed.

They went into the living room and all sat down. Father prayed, "Dear Father in heaven, please help us find T-Bone. We know that You have Your eye on him right now, and we pray that You will return him to us safe and sound. We thank You. We pray in the name of Jesus. Amen."

"Amen," everyone repeated.

They felt better. God was in charge, and He would rescue T-Bone. Mother got up and heated dinner. Alex and Rudy set the table. Barbara poured the drinks.

As they sat down to a late dinner, they were all quiet, each one thinking his or her own thoughts about T-Bone. Alex could only pray over and over to herself, *Please, Lord Jesus, help us find T-Bone.*

Toward the end of the dinner, it looked as if their prayers had been answered. The telephone rang. Father picked it up. He listened for a moment, and a look of joy lit up his face. He wrote something down on a piece of paper and hung up the telephone.

"T-Bone has been found!" he announced happily.

"YIPPEE!" they all cried.

"Who found him?" Mother asked.

"Some lady named Mrs. Steepleton. She sounded rather old. I think she said that T-Bone was in her backyard. She was a little hard to understand," Father shrugged. "I have the address right here. I don't suppose anyone would want to go with me to get T-Bone?" He winked at Mother.

"We do!" Alex, Rudy, and Barbara all cried at once. Mother said she was going, too.

They left the dinner dishes on the table and rushed out to the van. Father drove to Mrs. Steepleton's house. When they got there, they walked up to the front door and rang the bell.

"Oh, dear," Mrs. Steepleton cried as soon as she opened the door. "The most terrible thing has happened. I had your poor dog in the backyard, and I came inside to call you and to get him some water. But when I went back outside, he was gone! He must have pushed the gate open. It doesn't latch very well anymore. I'm terribly sorry."

"Oh, no!" Alex's family cried. They went around to Mrs. Steepleton's backyard. The gate was standing wide open. T-Bone was gone again!

"Let's all call him," Father suggested. "He may still be close by and hear us."

"T-BONE!" they shouted and shouted in every direction. They walked up and down the dark neighborhood calling and whistling. But nothing happened. No familiar bark met their ears. No familiar shape ran to greet them.

After about an hour, the family told Mrs. Steepleton good-bye and climbed back into the van. Father drove slowly up and down the neighborhood streets. Alex and Rudy hung out the windows and called for T-Bone. There was no sign of the dog. All they could do was turn around and go home.

It was quite late when they got back home, so Alex got ready for bed. Before getting into her bed, she knelt beside it and prayed, "Dear Lord Jesus, I know that You can do anything. Please find T-Bone and bring him home. I miss him a lot. I pray in Your name. Amen."

CHAPTER 3

Trouble with Eddie

    Alex had a hard time going to sleep that night. She missed T-Bone. He always slept on her bed. Now the bed seemed so empty without the big dog. Her cat, Tuna, helped make up for T-Bone's absence. The cat curled up beside her. Alex buried her face in Tuna's soft gray fur and cried herself to sleep.

    Toward the end of the night, Alex awoke from a strange dream. She had dreamed that T-Bone was with her at softball practice. Alex hit a ball just as hard as Rachel had, and it soared over the school fence and into the window of a house. In Alex's dream, T-Bone jumped through the window after the ball, but he couldn't get back out. He barked and barked. Alex called him, but he was too afraid to jump back out the window. All he could do was look at her and bark.

Alex shuddered as she remembered the dream. It had seemed so real. She wiggled down under the covers and put her arm around Tuna. Alex closed her eyes and began to drop off to sleep, when suddenly she heard a noise downstairs.

Bang, bang, bang! went the noise. It stopped for a moment and then started again. Bang, bang, bang . . . bang, bang!

Alex sat straight up in bed. What was that?

"Meow!" cried Tuna as she jumped off the bed.

"What is it, Tuna?" Alex asked the cat.

"Meow," Tuna answered and ran out of Alex's room to the top of the stairs. Alex could not see the gray cat in the shadows but could hear her cry, "Meow-ow-ow-ow!" all the way down the stairs. It was the same kind of excited cry Tuna made when Mother opened a can of tuna.

Why was Tuna excited? What was that noise downstairs? Alex decided she had to go see. She groped her way down the dark, winding stairway.

Bang, bang, bang! There it was again. Something or someone was hitting the front door. Alex froze in the middle of the stairs. What should she do? Go back up and get her father? Go down and peek out a window?

Taking a deep breath, Alex inched her way down the stairs. She would look out the peephole in the door. If there were anything dangerous outside, she could run back upstairs and get her parents.

Cautiously, Alex descended the last few steps and moved to the front door. On tiptoe, she squinted through the peephole. Alex could see nothing outside but vague outlines of shadows. She blinked and was about to squint with her other eye when, suddenly, someone touched her from behind!

"Ahhhhhh!" Alex screamed as she felt a hand on her shoulder. Before stopping to think, Alex kicked as hard as she could backward, slamming her leg into someone's knee.

"Ow!" cried a familiar voice. "Take it easy, Firecracker!"

"Dad?" Alex choked. She was so frightened, her breath came out in gasps.

"Calm down, honey," her father wrapped his arms around her. "It's just me. I thought I heard a noise down here."

"Me, too," Alex whispered. "I thought I heard someone banging at the front door."

Just then, the noise sounded again. Bang, bang, bang! It was accompanied by a low whine and then a bark.

Father and Alex jumped at the noise. They yanked open the front door. What they saw on the front porch made them cry out with joy.

Right before their eyes was T-Bone! As soon as he saw them, the big dog barked

happily. He pawed at the screen door,
trying to get in. Bang, bang, bang! The
door rattled loudly.

"So that's the noise that woke me up!"
Alex exclaimed. "It was T-Bone trying to
open the door!"

Father opened the screen door. T-Bone
leaped into Alex's open arms. Alex fell
backward onto the hallway floor. T-Bone
licked her face and neck furiously.

Father joined T-Bone and Alex on the
floor. They laughed and laughed as T-Bone

jumped from one to the other.

"What's going on down there?" asked a voice from the top of the stairway.

"Come down and find out!" Alex called up happily.

The stairway creaked as Mother tromped down the steps. Her face lit up at the sight of the black dog frolicking in the hallway.

"T-Bone!" Mother cried. She hurried down the last steps. The big dog rushed into Mother's arms just as he had rushed into Alex's and Father's arms.

"Ahhhh!" Mother cried as she fell back onto the bottom step. She laughed and hugged T-Bone.

"Well, I guess T-Bone found his way home," Alex said happily to Father.

"I guess he did, Firecracker," Father replied.

They all laughed as T-Bone looked at them happily.

"I'm sure God helped him find his way home," said Alex. "I prayed for him again when I went to bed."

"I think we should thank God for bringing our dog home, don't you?" Father asked.

"Yes," Mother and Alex agreed.

They bowed their heads. This time, Mother prayed. "Thank You, heavenly Father. You have shown Your great love for us by finding T-Bone and bringing him home. We are grateful to You. We pray in the name of Jesus. Amen."

After the prayer, Mother decided she would start the coffee brewing. It was almost time to get up anyway.

Alex, Father, and T-Bone followed her into the kitchen. It was then that Father noticed T-Bone was limping.

"What's the matter, Fella?" Father asked, concern in his voice. He squatted down in front of the dog.

T-Bone whined and placed his hurt paw on Father's knee. It was the right front paw.

Father examined the paw. "Oh, ho!" he

exclaimed as he discovered something embedded in between the pads of T-Bone's paw. "It's a thorn," he told Mother and Alex.

"Aw, poor puppy," Alex petted T-Bone's head. She got a grateful lick in return.

Father cleaned T-Bone's paw then tried to pull out the thorn with his fingers, but he couldn't budge it.

"I better get the tweezers," he decided. He sent Alex upstairs to get some hydrogen peroxide and cotton balls.

When they were ready, Alex helped steady T-Bone's paw while Father pulled at the thorn with the tweezers. It was stubborn. Finally, with a big jerk, the thorn came out. T-Bone yelped but got so much loving that he was soon wagging his tail. Father dripped hydrogen peroxide into the wound.

After Father was finished, Mother gave T-Bone some food and water. The dog lapped and lapped at the water. He ate the food hungrily. Then he sprawled on the kitchen rug in front of the sink for a nap.

"That figures!" Mother exclaimed. She had to step over the dog to fill the coffeepot with water.

Alex and Father laughed. "It's his favorite spot for a nap."

Alex skipped upstairs to get ready for school. The sun was just coming up. But even though it was early and Alex had not gone to sleep until late the night before, she didn't care. T-Bone was back home, and that was all that mattered.

On the way to school, Alex told her friends about T-Bone's adventures the night before.

"I can't believe Eddie Thompson did such a rotten thing as letting T-Bone into the creek!" Janie cried disgustedly.

"I can," Alex replied. "Eddie is a jerk!"

"Weren't you terribly worried?" Julie asked Alex.

"Sure. That's why we kept driving

47

around and calling for T-Bone," Alex replied.

"That's kind of neat that he found his own way home," Lorraine observed. "It's just like in the movies."

"Yeah," Alex agreed. "We oughta put T-Bone on film."

The others laughed.

Upon entering the classroom, Alex greeted Rachel and told her that T-Bone had been found. She did her best to ignore Eddie and his friends. She did not want to get into any fights.

At recess time, Alex asked Rachel if she would like to catch some balls. Rachel eagerly agreed. Alex got a softball and bat from her teacher. They walked to the diamond, where their friends joined them.

Soon they had a lively practice going. The other girls would take turns batting while Alex pitched and Rachel caught. Even without a glove, Rachel was a good catcher.

Everything went well until the boys

showed up. Rachel was taking her turn at bat. Julie had taken over catching. Alex threw one straight down the middle. Rachel, nervous because the boys were watching her, swung over it.

"Ha!" Eddie called out. "Strike one!"

Alex frowned. She threw another ball to Rachel. This time Rachel swung under it.

"Strike two!" Eddie sneered. The other boys hooted and hollered.

Alex glared at Eddie. She yelled at Rachel, "Come on, you can do it!" and then remembered that Rachel couldn't hear her. She wondered from how far away Rachel could read lips. If only Alex knew sign language like the police officer they had met the other day.

Alex warmed up and threw another pitch. It was too high, but Rachel, now completely upset by the boys, swung anyway and missed.

"Strike three!" Eddie called out triumphantly. "Maybe you'd like to pitch to a real batter?" he jeered and ran onto the field swinging a make-believe bat.

"Get outta here," Alex yelled at Eddie.

"Make me!" Eddie yelled back.

Alex clenched her fists and stomped toward Eddie. She was so angry at him that she might have punched him if Janie and Julie hadn't grabbed her and turned her around.

"Come on," they told her firmly as they marched her off the softball diamond and up toward the school building. Rachel and Lorraine followed behind with the bat and ball.

When the bell rang to go back inside, Alex had not calmed down very much. She was still mad at Eddie. So were the other girls. They ignored him and the other boys as best they could when they filed inside the school building.

Eddie grinned at Alex and purposely knocked into her desk on the way to his desk. He sat down in his desk behind Rachel and banged his foot against her chair. Rachel ignored him. He then moved the front of his desk smack up against the back of her chair. Alex watched helplessly as Eddie began shoving Rachel and her chair forward.

Finally, Rachel could stand it no longer. Right in the middle of Mrs. Shivers's American history lesson, Rachel squeezed out of her chair, grabbed Eddie's desk and shoved it backward as hard as she could. The desk slammed into Eddie, knocking him and the chair over backward onto the floor.

The classroom exploded with laughter and cheers when Eddie hit the floor. Alex cheered the loudest. But her cheering stopped when she caught sight of Rachel's grief-stricken face. Holding both hands to cover her face, Rachel rushed out of the classroom. Alex got up and followed her.

Out in the hallway, Rachel leaned against the wall and sobbed and sobbed. Alex tried her best to comfort her. She put her hand on Rachel's shoulder to let her know that she had a friend nearby.

In the background, Alex could hear Mrs. Shivers restore order to the classroom. Soon the teacher came out and stood on the other side of Rachel. She put her arm around Rachel.

Alex told Mrs. Shivers how Eddie Thompson had tormented Rachel by dropping books behind her and blowing whistles at her. She told her how Eddie had made fun of Rachel on the softball field and had shoved his desk into her chair.

Mrs. Shivers shook her head in sympathy. She finally managed to stop Rachel's crying. She and Alex told Rachel not to worry, that everything was okay.

Alex and Rachel went back into the classroom. Mrs. Shivers called Eddie out into the hall. After a while, the teacher returned alone. Alex did not see Eddie for the rest of the day, and she was glad. She did not care if she ever saw Eddie Thompson again in her whole life.

CHAPTER 4

A Boy and a Giant

"LADIES AND GENTLEMEN! FIND YOUR SEATS QUICKLY! THE BIG SHOW IS ABOUT TO BEGIN!" Rudy announced loudly. He wore an old topcoat and a hat of Father's. In his hand was a pretend microphone.

Father and Mother hurried to take their seats in the family room. It was Treasure Hunt night. Once a week, the family gathered for an evening of storytelling. The stories were from the Bible. As the family talked about the stories, they learned valuable lessons for their own lives. This was the treasure they hunted.

Tonight, however, was special. Barbara, Alex, Rudy, and T-Bone were acting out a story from the Bible.

"Tonight's show is called 'David, the Giant Killer,'" Rudy announced. "Let the show begin!" He hurried out of the room.

Barbara was the first actor to appear "onstage." She stomped into the family room waving a plastic sword. She wore one of Father's bathrobes tied around the middle with a belt. Sandals were on her feet. Her face was set in a mean-looking scowl. Barbara was Goliath, the mean giant.

"I CHALLENGE YOU, ISRAEL!" Barbara cried out loudly. "SEND ME A MAN TO FIGHT. IF HE IS ABLE TO KILL ME, THEN WE, THE PHILISTINES, WILL BECOME YOUR SERVANTS. BUT IF I KILL HIM, THEN ISRAEL WILL BE OUR SERVANTS!"

Barbara stood in the middle of the room and looked around for someone to fight.

Alex entered the room and stayed off to one side. She was dressed in a long, flowing robe and had a gold-colored crown on her head. She began to speak, "I am King Saul, King of Israel. I am looking for a volunteer to fight the giant, Goliath. Are there any volunteers?" Alex looked behind a door and under the sofa. Mother and Father laughed.

"WHO WILL FIGHT ME?" Barbara roared again. "IS THERE NO ONE IN ISRAEL BRAVE ENOUGH TO GO AGAINST GOLIATH?"

"Oh, dear, oh, dear," Alex, as King Saul, wrung her hands. "Isn't there anyone in my army who will fight this giant?"

"I will!" Rudy leapt into the room. He had made a quick costume change, and now he, too, was dressed in a bathrobe, belted around the middle, and had sandals on his feet. He knelt before King Saul and said, "I, your servant, will go and fight this Philistine giant."

"Who are you?" King Saul asked.

"My name is David," Rudy answered. "I am a shepherd boy, the son of Jesse."

"But you can't fight the giant," King Saul waved her arms frantically. "You are just a boy!"

"But I am very brave," replied David. "Let me show you." At this, Rudy whistled for T-Bone. The big dog bounded into the room.

David said to King Saul, "Once when I was looking after my father's sheep a lion came and took away a lamb. I attacked the lion and rescued the lamb." David grabbed T-Bone and wrestled with him. Then he said, "When the lion rose against me, I struck and killed him." David pretended to strike T-Bone. He made T-Bone lie down on the floor.

Mother and Father applauded the bravery of David. They also clapped for T-Bone and his performance.

"I also have killed a bear in the same

way," David told King Saul. "The Lord helped me win against the lion and the bear. He will also help me win against this Philistine giant."

"Very well," said King Saul. "Do you have any armor to wear?"

"No, I have no armor," replied David.

"Then let me put my armor on you." King Saul grabbed an old football helmet from behind a chair. "Here," said the king, "try on this helmet."

As soon as King Saul placed the helmet on his head, David staggered and fell down. "It's too heavy," he gasped, struggling to pull it off. "I cannot wear your armor. I will fight the giant with my sling and stones."

Taking a pretend slingshot and some stones in his hands, David approached the giant.

"HA, HA, HA!" Goliath roared when David approached. "You are just a puny kid. You cannot fight me!"

David called to the giant, "You come to

me with a sword and a spear, but I come to you in the name of the Lord. Today the Lord will deliver you into my hands, and everyone will know that there is a God in Israel!"

The giant let out an angry roar and stomped toward David. David took a pretend stone and slung it at the giant. It hit the giant on the forehead, and she fell to the ground. David had won!

Father and Mother clapped their hands as first Rudy, then Alex took their bows. Barbara struggled to her feet and also received applause.

"Very good, very good!" Father and Mother praised their children. "That's one of my favorite stories in the Bible," said Father. "I think you put on a very good performance. Can you tell me why, out of all the strong men in Israel's army, God picked a young boy like David to fight the giant?"

Alex, Rudy, and Barbara stared at one another with puzzled looks on their faces.

Finally, Rudy said, "Well, because he was brave and he had already killed a lion and a bear!"

Father chuckled, "No, it was a little more than just being brave."

Mother gave them a helpful hint, "What did David say about killing the lion and the bear? Who helped him do it?"

"Oh, yeah," said Rudy. "He said that the Lord helped him win against the lion and the bear."

"That's right," smiled Mother. "David

always relied on the Lord to help him do things. He was strong in the Lord."

"What was God's message when He helped David win against the giant?" asked Father.

"God was saying it didn't matter that David was small. He was going to win against the giant because he was fighting for God's army," Alex answered.

"Very good, Firecracker," Father used her nickname. "David couldn't have won that battle all by himself. The Lord helped him win so everyone would know that the Lord delivers His people from their enemies."

"Even when they are giants," put in Rudy.

"That's right," Father smiled. "Now let me ask you another question. Does anybody know what a 'mission' is?"

"Is it like a missionary who goes to other countries to tell people about Jesus?" Alex asked.

"Close," answered Father.

"A mission is a kind of church," suggested Barbara.

"Nah, it means outer space," cried Rudy. "You know, like a mission to the moon."

They all laughed.

"Actually, Rudy is the closest to the right answer," Father said. "When people go on a mission to the moon, they have a specific reason for going. Maybe it's to collect rocks or explore craters. Whatever it is, they have a purpose for going to the moon. That purpose is called their mission.

"David was the same way," Father went on. "He wasn't just out to kill a giant. He had a bigger mission. His mission was to let others know that there was a God in Israel and that God would deliver His people from their enemy. Killing Goliath was one part of David's big mission.

"Now what about you and me?" Father asked his children. "Will God give us a mission like He gave to David? Are we called to be God's children for a purpose?"

"I'm sure we must be," replied Alex. "I just don't know what mine is yet."

Mother patted her hand. "You will know someday, Alex. Ask God to show you your mission in life. We all have purpose. God made each of us for a reason. We need to find that reason and then go for it. We need to achieve our mission. There is no greater success than that."

"David was successful," commented Barbara. "He killed the giant."

"Yes, he did," Father nodded, "and later in his life, he became king of Israel even though he started out as only a shepherd boy."

"That's really a neat mission," exclaimed Alex.

"God has a neat mission for each of us," said Father. "We need to discover what He has for our lives."

"That's kind of exciting to think about," said Alex. "I wonder what my mission will be."

"Me, too," added Barbara.

"I know what I want my mission to be!" announced Rudy.

"What's that?" they all asked.

Rudy slung another pretend stone. "I hope my mission is just like David's—to kill a big, bad giant for God!"

CHAPTER 5

Crocodile Meatloaf

The next day at school, Alex stayed by Rachel's side. If Eddie Thompson and his friends so much as looked in their direction, Alex would glare at them and shake her fist in warning. No one dared to approach the two girls.

That evening, after softball practice and before dinner, Alex asked her father a question.

"Dad, is it possible to have a little mission even before you know what your big mission is?"

"Yes, I think so, Firecracker," Father replied. "What kind of little mission are you talking about?"

"Well," Alex frowned. "I think that God wants me to help Rachel. She's having a tough time at school with the boys." Alex told her father about Eddie and his friends teasing Rachel. "So," she continued, "I thought about David and Goliath and what you said about having a mission, and I wondered if helping Rachel could be my little mission right now."

"I think that would be a wonderful mission, Firecracker," Father patted Alex's shoulder. "But I would not call that a little mission. I think it's part of your big mission."

"What's my big mission?" Alex asked.

"I think you have been specially called by God to minister to people," answered Father.

"Minister to people?" asked Alex. "What does that mean?"

"It means to love people and to help them in whatever way they need help," Father answered.

"Oh," Alex was pleased. "That's a

really neat mission, isn't it?"

"The best," smiled Father, "and while you're helping people, you can tell them about Jesus."

"Yeah," Alex agreed. "Brussels sprouts! Maybe I'll be a missionary someday and go to another country—maybe even a country in Africa!"

"I wouldn't be surprised," Father nodded. Then he winked. "Maybe you'll end up in a grass hut deep in some jungle eating crocodile meat for breakfast!"

"Oh, Dad!" Alex wrinkled her nose in disgust. "Well," she added brightly, "you and Mom can visit me at Christmas and we'll have the specialty of the house."

"What's that?" Father asked.

"Crocodile meatloaf!" Alex replied with a grin.

"Thanks a lot!" Father laughed.

At the dinner table, Alex and Father told the rest of the family how Alex was going to live in Africa and eat crocodile meatloaf.

"I'm going to be the Great Crocodile Meatloaf Missionary," Alex laughed.

"Awesome!" shouted Rudy. "Can I come live with you?"

"Oh, how disgusting!" cried Barbara. She and Mother made faces at Alex.

After dinner, Alex asked Father if he would drive her over to Rachel's house. Rachel had left her math book on the bench at ball practice and forgot to take it home. Alex had rescued the book. Because they had a math test the next day, Alex was sure that Rachel would need the book that night.

"Why, of course, I'll drive you to Rachel's house," Father told Alex.

"Oh, let me drive, PLEASE!" Barbara suddenly cried. Barbara was just learning to drive. She would turn sixteen later on in the year.

"Well, I don't know," Father teased.

"Oh, come on, Dad," Barbara pleaded. "Can I drive the van?"

"No, I don't think you should drive the

van until you've had more experience," said Father. "It's too hard to see out of it. You can drive my car instead."

"Okay," said Barbara. "Can we drive past Michael's house on the way home?" Barbara asked a moment later. "I want to show him how I can drive."

Alex rolled her eyes. Barbara had a new boyfriend named Michael. She was always talking about Michael this or Michael that. Alex tried not to pay much attention to Barbara's boyfriends. She seemed to have a new one every month.

"Okay," Father smiled at his older daughter. "We can drive past Michael's house on the way home."

Barbara leaped in the air and ran to get her own set of car keys. Alex sighed and rolled her eyes at Father. How could Barbara be so excited about boys? All the boys in Alex's sixth-grade class were disgusting and had been since third grade. "Boys must change a lot between sixth grade and high school," Alex told

Father. "At least I hope so."

Father laughed and walked outside with his two daughters. Alex climbed in the backseat of Father's car while Barbara and Father sat up front. Barbara started the car and backed it smoothly out of the driveway. Alex was impressed. Her sister was improving.

They made it to Rachel's house with no trouble at all. Barbara handled the car skillfully all the way there. Rachel was grateful to Alex for bringing her math book to her. Alex waved good-bye to Rachel, and they started off for Michael's house. He did not live very far away. When they reached his house, Barbara pulled into the driveway and honked. Michael and his family came outside.

Father talked to Michael's parents while Barbara and Michael flirted with each other. Alex felt awkward and completely left out of the conversation. It didn't last long, however. Soon Father said it was time to go.

They all said good-bye. Barbara began to back the car out of the driveway. Trying to impress Michael and his parents, Barbara drove a little too fast. The car shot out of the driveway. Barbara swerved to the right when she should have angled to the left. Before Father could stop her, Barbara backed into the mailbox that stood a few feet away from the driveway. It fell over and was crushed by the right rear tire. The tire also flattened the flower garden that Michael's mother had planted around the mailbox.

"Stop the car!" Father cried in alarm.

Barbara jerked to a stop. Her face was white, and she looked about ready to cry.

Father leapt out of the car to inspect the damage. Alex followed him. Michael and his parents ran to the end of the driveway.

"Oh, dear!" Michael's mother exclaimed when she saw the crushed mailbox and flowers.

"I'm terribly sorry," Father apologized.

"Barbara hasn't had much experience backing up the car."

Tears streamed down Barbara's face as she clutched the steering wheel.

"Hey, it's okay," Michael told her awkwardly. He reached in through the car window and patted her shoulder.

"I'll buy you a new mailbox," Father offered Michael's parents, "and new flowers, of course," he added quickly.

"That's okay," Michael's father replied. "Think nothing of it. I hope your car isn't damaged from the impact."

Father inspected the rear of his car. There were only a few scratches on the bumper. When he got back in the car, he exchanged places with Barbara. Father carefully inched the car out of the flower garden and back onto the driveway. After assuring Michael's family that he would pay for the damage, he drove out of the driveway and onto the street.

As soon as they turned the corner, Father pulled over to the edge of the road and stopped the car. He tried to give Barbara a stern look, but his face soon broke into a grin. It wasn't long before all three of them were laughing.

"I'm sure you will never forget how you knocked over your boyfriend's mailbox the first time you drove a car to his house!" Father told Barbara.

"I *know* I'll never forget it," Barbara agreed, wiping the laughter tears from her eyes. "Thanks for not getting mad. Thanks for understanding, Dad," she told him.

"Sure, honey," Father moved over to sit by Barbara. He put an arm around her shoulders. "I have a confession to make," he told her and Alex.

"What?" the girls asked.

Father grinned broadly. "When I was Barbara's age, I did the same thing, only I didn't just hit a mailbox. I wiped out a picket fence and a statue of a donkey!"

Barbara and Alex howled with laughter. "How'd you do that?" they asked between gulps of air.

"Well, I hadn't been driving very long, and I turned a corner a little too fast and ended up in the neighbor's yard instead of the street," Father replied sheepishly. "So you see, I can't yell at you too much," he told Barbara.

"Did you get into trouble?" Alex asked.

"Of course I did," Father answered. "I had to pay for the damage and put up a new fence."

"What about the donkey statue?" Alex giggled.

"Actually, I think the neighbors would have been happy to see it go. The yard was full of those statues," said Father. "But I replaced it just the same."

"I'll pay for the mailbox and flowers that I hit," offered Barbara.

"Okay," Father nodded, "but first let's see how much our insurance will pay for it. Do you want to drive home?"

"You mean you'll trust me with the car again?" Barbara asked hopefully.

"I believe in second chances," Father smiled. He got out of the car and exchanged places once again with Barbara.

Alex watched her sister happily head the car for home. Alex was glad her father had not been mad at Barbara for hitting the mailbox. It was good to know that Father was so understanding. After all, Alex might accidentally back into something when she began to drive. At least she knew one thing. She would watch out for mailboxes, picket fences, and donkey statues.

CHAPTER 6

Search for Rachel

The next Friday, Mrs. Shivers took the class on a field trip. They were to visit a miniature farm set up on the outskirts of suburban Kansas City.

It was a beautiful spring day, sunny and unusually warm. Alex enjoyed the long bus ride out to the farm. She sat with Rachel and Janie. Julie and Lorraine sat behind them. Because Mrs. Shivers had suggested they wear hats to protect their faces from the bright Kansas sunshine, the girls wore an assortment of colorful caps on their heads. Alex wore the traditional blue identified with the Kansas City Royals baseball team, while Rachel wore a bright neon pink cap.

Because the girls sat at the front of the bus and Eddie and his friends sat at the back of the bus, the girls enjoyed a peaceful trip.

The boys, however, did not enjoy the ride. They had not counted on Mrs. Shivers sitting at the back of the bus. Alex could not keep from grinning when Mrs. Shivers sat next to Eddie, but Alex felt sorry for Mrs. Shivers. Nobody deserved a bus ride next to Eddie Thompson!

The bus wound its way through the countryside. Finally, it pulled into a long driveway with rows of fruit trees on each side. The bus pulled up into a circular parking area and the children got out. They followed a sidewalk to a large, grassy area surrounded by farm buildings. Alex could see a chicken coop, a red barn and silo, a horse corral, a tack house, and an old farmhouse. But what really caught everyone's attention was a fenced-in area containing two large and one small buffalo!

Alex stared at the shaggy animals. They did not seem particularly happy to see the group of noisy children. One of the big animals gave a terrific bellow.

"Ahhhhh!" the children cried in surprise. Even Mrs. Shivers looked apprehensive.

"QUIET DOWN, PECOS!" a young woman suddenly shouted. She had just come out of the farmhouse. She walked over to the buffalo pen and said, "These are our guests, Pecos. You should have better manners."

The children laughed. Again, the buffalo bellowed.

"I'm afraid we'll just have to put up with Pecos today," the young woman addressed the group of children and Mrs. Shivers. "He's a bit touchy around his wife and new baby. That's his wife, Calamity, and his baby, Hop-along."

Everyone laughed again and several made "oooohs" and "ahhhhs" at baby Hop-along. His coat was soft and downy compared to the rough, shaggy coats of his parents.

"My name is Molly," the young woman introduced herself to the class. "I'll be your guide for today. We have a few rules here at the farm. The number-one rule is that no one is allowed inside the buffalo fence. Also, do not lean against the fence. Pecos has been known to charge into it!"

Molly said a few more things then gave the children time to watch Pecos and his family. The group of children was noisy. The boys were especially troublesome. Eddie and his friends waved their arms at Pecos, hoping to make him charge the fence. The big buffalo held his head down and stared at the boys.

Alex and her friends also watched the buffalo. Rachel seemed especially interested in the baby buffalo. She tried her best to coax Hop-along to the fence.

Quite suddenly, out of the corner of her eye, Alex saw the big buffalo come to life. Head down and snorting, Pecos ran full speed at the fence! WHAM! Shock waves ran up and down the entire length of the fence.

"WOW!" everyone gasped.

Molly gathered the children together and started them on the tour of the barnyard. Alex had to pull Rachel away from the buffalo pen and baby Hop-along.

The children visited the chicken coop and saw the rows of nests set on wooden planks, reaching several levels high. The hens squawked and flapped their wings at the visitors. They made an awful racket.

When they visited the big barn, the children climbed up to the hayloft. A huge slide with a big hump in its middle ran from the hayloft down to the ground. There was also a giant rope swing that hung from the rafters of the barn.

Molly climbed to the hayloft to supervise the slide. Mrs. Shivers stayed on the ground to help with the swing.

While Alex liked both the swing and the slide, her favorite was the rope swing. It soared so far and so high that she felt butterflies in her stomach.

Finally, Molly led them to the farmhouse for lunch. Afterward, the children had free time. They could roam the barnyard and surrounding areas to do what they liked.

"Can we go down to the pond?" Alex asked Molly. She had seen a duck pond not too far from the barn. It looked like a fun place to explore.

"Why, sure," Molly encouraged Alex. "Go on down to the duck pond. It's a fun place."

Alex, Rachel, Janie, Julie, and Lorraine started off for the pond, but soon Rachel left the group to return to the buffalo pen. She wanted to watch baby Hop-along.

"Okay," Alex told Rachel. "We'll come back to the buffalo pen and get you later. Be careful of Pecos," she added.

Rachel grinned and waved good-bye.

The duck pond was cool and shaded. Alex and her friends strolled around the pond in contentment. They shut out the distant clamor and noise from their classmates.

"This is great," Alex told her friends. She plopped down at the edge of the pond and relaxed in the cool shade.

"I'm gonna put my feet in the water," announced Janie. She began taking off her shoes and socks.

"Great idea!" the others followed her example.

"Brussels sprouts, that's cold!" Alex exclaimed as she gingerly eased one foot after the other into the water.

She and her friends sat side by side with their feet in the water, watching the ducks. No one noticed the army of crawdads circling the girls' bare toes until it attacked!

"YEOUCH!" Alex suddenly cried. Crawdads had attached themselves to both of her feet. Alex kicked frantically. The crawdads came loose and fell back into the water.

The other girls were busy kicking their feet too. One giant crawdad hung from Janie's toe and would not let go.

"GET IT OFF! GET IT OFF!" Janie screamed at the top of her lungs. Alex looked around and found a long stick. She jabbed at Janie's crawdad, knocking it into the water.

"Oh, thank you, Alex!" Janie gasped.

The girls scooted back away from the edge of the pond, dragging their shoes and socks with them. It was then that

Janie noticed one of her tennis shoes was missing.

"Maybe you knocked it into the water when you were kicking at the crawdad," Alex suggested.

The girls carefully leaned over the edge of the pond. Because the water was clear and not very deep, they soon located the shoe. It rested at the bottom of the pond. A swarm of crawdads covered it.

"Forget it!" Janie decided. "I'm not trying to get it."

"You mean you're going to go home without a shoe?"

"I guess so," Janie replied. "There's no way to get my shoe without getting attacked by those horrid crawdads."

"Maybe there is," Alex said thoughtfully. She grabbed a stick. Lowering it into the water, Alex fished for Janie's shoe. It was a hard task. The shoe was too heavy with water and so unbalanced that it would not stay on the end of the stick but fell back into the water. Alex tried again and again. Finally she was able to haul in the shoe. Carefully, she poured out the water, along with two crawdads.

"Oh, how disgusting!" Janie wrinkled her nose at the crawdads. After first making sure there were no other crawdads in the shoe, she gingerly picked it up and held it as far away from her as possible.

Watching Janie, Alex began to laugh. So did the others. Finally, even Janie joined in. They laughed and laughed about their adventure with the crawdads.

Having had enough of the duck pond, the girls climbed the sloping hill back to the barnyard. When they got there, they told Molly what had happened. She laughed and took them to the farmhouse where she rinsed out the shoe and then hung it out on the clothesline to dry. As it was a sunny, windy day, Molly assured Janie that it would dry quickly.

Alex went to tell Rachel that they were back from the duck pond, but

Rachel was not at the buffalo pen. She was not in the barn, either. Alex checked the other farm buildings. Rachel was nowhere in sight.

Becoming concerned, Alex asked Mrs. Shivers if she had seen Rachel. Mrs. Shivers had not. Alex and her friends searched for Rachel. But Rachel could not be found. Alex became very worried. So did Mrs. Shivers. She assembled all the children in the barnyard and asked if anyone knew where Rachel was. No one did. This time, everyone helped look for Rachel. It was a silent search. No one called for Rachel because she could not hear them call her name.

After fifteen minutes, everyone reported back to Mrs. Shivers. No one had found her. Rachel was lost!

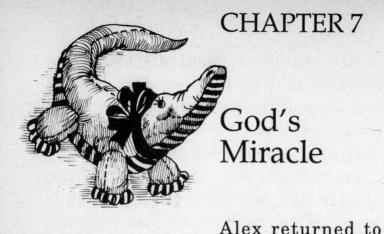

CHAPTER 7

God's Miracle

Alex returned to the buffalo pen one more time. That was the last place they knew that Rachel had visited.

Leaning against the fence and staring into the pen, Alex was startled to see a familiar pink object lying several feet inside the pen. It was Rachel's cap! But what was it doing inside the buffalo pen?

Just at that moment, a voice sounded in her ear, "Uh, Alex, can I talk to you for a minute?"

Surprised, Alex turned to see Eddie Thompson standing behind her.

"What do you want?" Alex asked Eddie suspiciously.

"Uh, it's about Rachel," Eddie began awkwardly. "I, uh, think it's my fault that she ran away and got lost."

"What?" Alex angrily exclaimed. "What did you do to her?"

For once, Eddie did not lash back at Alex. He seemed very worried about Rachel.

"We were just messing around," Eddie tried to explain. "I threw her cap into the buffalo pen but, it was just for a joke. I didn't mean to make her run away and get lost. I'm really sorry."

Alex tapped her foot and stared at Eddie. "Why are you always picking on Rachel?" she finally asked.

"I dunno," Eddie stared at the ground. "It all started out as fun. I guess we got too carried away. If we find Rachel, I'd just like to be friends."

"Friends!" Alex's mouth dropped open in surprise. Was this really Eddie? "Okay, we'll try and be friends," she decided, "but first we gotta find Rachel. Did you see which way she went?"

"Yeah, she went off that way," Eddie pointed toward a trail that ran behind the buffalo pen and into a small stand of woods. "But I already looked down that trail and couldn't find her."

"Let's look again," Alex suggested. "Come on!"

By now, several of Eddie's friends and Alex's friends had joined them. The group began to move toward the woods.

"Janie, go tell Mrs. Shivers where we're going," Alex directed. Janie ran off to find the teacher.

As they followed the trail through the woods, the children looked behind bushes and trees. They walked several yards but there was still no trace of Rachel. Alex began to despair. Where was Rachel? How would they ever find her? There were so many places for her to hide. In desperation, she turned to the one person who could help.

"Dear Lord Jesus," she prayed,

"please help us find Rachel. We need Your help. I pray in Your name. Amen."

As Alex prayed, she lifted her eyes toward heaven. In doing so, she suddenly noticed a bright pink object high up in a tree. What was that? Alex stared intently at the top of the tall tree. It was a pink shirt! Alex was able to pick out an arm and then a familiar face from among the branches and leaves in the tree. It was Rachel!

"THERE SHE IS!" Alex hollered to the rest of the group. She bounced up and down on the path in joy as she pointed to the top of the oak tree.

"WOW!" Eddie and the boys exclaimed when they saw how high Rachel had climbed. "How'd she get up there?"

"Climbed, of course," Alex shrugged. She could tell the boys were impressed.

"RACHEL! COME DOWN!" Alex called even though she knew Rachel couldn't hear her. She and the others moved to the base of Rachel's tree and motioned for her to come down. But Rachel only stared at them and refused to move.

"I suppose I'll have to climb up and get her," Alex decided. Being a tree climber herself, Alex really didn't mind the idea.

"No, you don't have to climb the tree," Eddie told Alex. "I should be the one to do it. After all, it's my fault Rachel went up there in the first place."

Alex could not argue with that. She watched as Eddie swung himself into the tree and climbed, branch by branch, up to Rachel.

Rachel did not move, but only glared at Eddie as he made his way toward her and finally stopped to sit on a branch right beneath her.

Alex watched as Eddie talked to Rachel. She and the others hoped that Eddie would convince Rachel to come down out of the tree.

"Thank You, Lord Jesus, for helping me find Rachel," Alex prayed. "Now please help us get her out of the tree and please help us all be friends, even the boys," she added. "I pray in Your name. Amen."

A minute or two later, Alex noticed that a smile had spread across Rachel's face. Together, Rachel and Eddie began the long climb down the tree.

Footsteps suddenly sounded on the trail as Janie, followed by Mrs. Shivers, burst into view.

"Oh, my goodness!" Mrs. Shivers exclaimed when she saw Rachel and Eddie up in the tree. "BE CAREFUL!" she called to them.

Mrs. Shivers waited until they were safely out of the tree and then asked Eddie and Rachel to explain why they were in the tree.

Rachel shrugged and lowered her eyes. She did not say a word. Eddie told the teacher how he had teased Rachel and thrown her cap into the buffalo pen, causing her to run away and climb the tree.

"Eddie Thompson! What am I going to do with you?" Mrs. Shivers exclaimed.

"But he did climb the tree and talk Rachel into coming down," Alex said in Eddie's behalf. "Doesn't that count for something?"

Mrs. Shivers looked at Alex in surprise. "Yes," she admitted and turned to Eddie and Rachel. "Does this mean that you two can be friends now?" she asked.

Rachel and Eddie exchanged an embarrassed glance. "I guess so," replied Eddie. Rachel nodded in agreement.

"Good!" said the teacher. "Then I suppose losing a cap and climbing a tree were worth it. Come on, children, it's time to get back on the bus to go home."

Everybody laughed happily and followed Mrs. Shivers back to the barnyard where the bus was waiting for them. When they passed the buffalo pen, they were surprised to see that baby Hop-along had taken a fancy to Rachel's cap. The little buffalo pranced around the pen tossing the cap in the air and catching it with his teeth.

"He plays like T-Bone did when he was a puppy!" Alex cried.

"Just let Hop-along keep my cap," Rachel told Molly. Rachel seemed pleased that she was able to give the baby buffalo a present.

Back on the bus, Alex asked Rachel what Eddie had said to her up in the tree.

"Oh, he just said he was sorry that he took my cap and he hoped we could stop fighting and be friends," Rachel replied.

"Brussels sprouts, that's amazing," Alex commented. She glanced back at Eddie. He was actually talking and laughing with Mrs. Shivers.

Alex shook her head and rolled her eyes to the ceiling. She had asked the Lord to make everyone friends and He had done so. Not only had He answered her prayer, but it seemed He also had turned Eddie Thompson into a normal, friendly person. That was a miracle!

The next week at school was much better for Alex and Rachel. The boys, especially Eddie, treated them as friends. There were no mean words and no fights.

The last day of the week was the best. Alex was so excited. She was having a slumber party that night. She planned the party for Rachel's benefit. Alex hoped that Rachel might become better friends with the other girls too. Her parents had agreed with her plan and allowed her to invite ten girls to the slumber party.

Alex rushed home from school to help her mother with the last minute preparations. Father came home with boxes of pizzas. At six-thirty, the doorbell began to ring. Alex took each guest down the stairs to the recreation room where they would all spend the night.

Before long, the party was in full swing. The girls devoured pizza and soda pop. Some challenged others to Ping-Pong games. Some just talked and giggled lots. Others played board games.

All of them were noisy.

Rachel joined Alex in several lively Ping-Pong games and had fun beating everyone at Monopoly. She looked like she was having a great time.

Rachel was not the only one enjoying herself. The black labrador, T-Bone, was having the time of his life. He thought the party was just for him. He joined in all the activities and was generally welcomed by the girls. T-Bone's favorite activity, of course, was helping finish off the pizza. No one could leave a piece of pizza unattended on the floor.

As soon as the pizza was gone, Alex carried down potato chips and bowls of popcorn. Even though they were stuffed with pizza, the girls munched on the new goodies eagerly.

Finally, around midnight, Mother and Father came downstairs to say good night. They urged the girls to unroll their sleeping bags and arrange them on the floor just in case they wanted to sleep sometime during the night.

The girls took their suggestion and even settled down to watch a movie. They picked *Sleeping Beauty* so they could "ooooh" and "ahhhh" at the handsome prince.

They weren't far into the movie when disaster struck. T-Bone had been eyeing a bowl of popcorn all evening. When the girls lay down on their sleeping bags to watch the movie, T-Bone decided that was his chance. The popcorn bowl sat on top of a TV tray. T-Bone, very quietly, climbed up on a stuffed chair next to the TV tray, leaned his front legs over the arm of the chair, and stuck his big nose into the bowl of popcorn.

Janie was the first one to notice T-Bone happily munching away. She giggled and pointed at the dog. When Alex saw him she yelled, "T-BONE! GET OUTTA THAT POPCORN!"

The sudden shout startled the dog. He lost his balance and fell headfirst into the bowl. The TV tray, the bowl of popcorn, and the dog all crashed to the floor.

"OH, NO!" Alex groaned. She switched off the movie and went to inspect the mess T-Bone had made.

"You mutt!" she told the dog. He hung his head and slinked off to a corner.

"I think we need a vacuum," Janie suggested when they tried to pick up the popcorn. "It would be much quicker."

"Good idea," Alex agreed. She ran upstairs and pulled the vacuum out of the closet next to the kitchen.

Plugging it in downstairs, Alex let Janie run the vacuum over the spilled popcorn. Janie was much better than Alex at that sort of thing and actually liked to do it.

Everything went just fine until the vacuum picked up something other than popcorn. They heard a funny-sounding CLINK! and then SHRIEEEEEK! the vacuum began to wail. A burning smell filled the air.

"QUICK! TURN IT OFF!" Alex cried. She helped Janie find the switch.

The girls looked at each other anxiously. Had they broken the vacuum cleaner?

"All we have to do is get out whatever made the clinking noise," Janie told Alex.

"And how do we do that?" Alex wanted to know.

"We just kind of shake it out," Janie told her. She heaved the vacuum onto its side and peered into the bottom of it. "There must be something stuck in the rollers," she decided.

Janie turned the vacuum cleaner upside down and shook it. Then she turned it right side up and shook it. She slammed it on its side a few times to try and dislodge the stuck item, but nothing fell out of the machine.

Alex hoped that Janie knew what she was doing. Her parents would not be happy if they had broken the vacuum cleaner.

"Let's try turning it on again," Janie finally suggested. "Maybe whatever it was shook loose and will go up into the bag."

Janie flipped the switch to the on position. Not only did the machine smoke and shriek, but it POPPED as well.

"AHHHHH!" cried Janie as dust and dirt blew up in her face. She had shaken the vacuum so much that the bag that held the dirt had been damaged. When she turned the machine back on, the force of air popped the bag and blew the dirt into her face.

"TURN IT OFF!" Janie hollered. She could not see to turn off the switch. Dust had blown into her eyes.

Alex yanked the cord out of the electric socket. The noise stopped and the dust slowly settled to the floor.

"Now what do we do?" Alex wanted to know.

"Take a bath!" Janie told her. She gave Alex a disgusted look and brushed the dust off of herself.

"I mean what do we do about the vacuum?" Alex insisted.

"I guess we oughta put another bag on it," said Janie.

"Oh, yeah," Alex nodded. "I know where Mom keeps the bags." She ran upstairs. T-Bone and several of the other girls followed, laughing and talking loudly.

"Shhhh!" Alex warned them. "My parents might hear you. I don't want them to come downstairs and see the mess."

The girls nodded and followed Alex silently as she once again made her way to the pantry and utility closet. She scanned the shelves for the package of vacuum cleaner bags. She spotted them high up on a shelf wedged between a stack of paper plates and a giant box of T-Bone's dog biscuits.

Without bothering to go get a step stool, Alex climbed on a lower shelf and then stretched for the bags. The shelves, however, were not made to stand on. The boards were not nailed in place but

only rested on their supports. When Alex clung to the top shelf, it suddenly pitched forward.

BANG! CRASH! Alex, the shelf, and all the items on the shelf crashed to the floor!

Alex lay sprawled on the floor of the closet, buried under a pile of paper plates and dog biscuits. Other items such as paper napkins, soap, and toothpicks littered the floor around her. The vacuum cleaner bags lay at her feet.

"Ohhhhh," moaned Alex. She sat up and rubbed her head. Then Alex heard the sound she had so dreaded to hear.

"ALEX!" called Mother. "What is going on down there?"

Alex and her friends froze as hurried footsteps ran down the stairs. Soon both parents came into view. They stared in disbelief at Alex as she sat in the closet covered with plates, dog biscuits, toothpicks, soap, and napkins.

"Uh, hi," Alex tried to smile. "Want a biscuit?"

CHAPTER 8

Caught in the Dark

"What happened?" Alex's parents demanded when they saw Alex and the mess that covered the closet floor.

"Well, the top shelf fell and so did everything else, including me," Alex tried to explain.

"Are you all right?" her parents asked anxiously.

"I think so," Alex replied a little doubtfully. She got to her feet slowly, letting the items in her lap fall to the floor. Father helped her out of the closet.

"Would you mind telling us why you were in the pantry in the first place?" Father asked.

"Well, uh, you see, I was looking for the vacuum cleaner bags, and I had to . . . " Alex began.

"Why the vacuum cleaner bags?" Mother interrupted.

"Well, T-Bone knocked over some popcorn, and we tried to vacuum it up but we ran over something. Anyway, the vacuum started burning and making this weird noise and Janie tried to fix it but she broke the bag and dust flew all over . . . " Alex stopped speaking. Horrified looks had spread over her parents' faces. Without waiting to hear another word, they rushed past Alex and down the basement stairs.

The vacuum still lay on its side in the middle of the room. A fine gray film of dust covered everything around it.

The girls watched anxiously as Father checked over the vacuum cleaner. When he shook it gently, they heard a faint clinking sound.

"Aha!" exclaimed Father. He reached

inside the bottom part of the vacuum and slowly turned the rollers. He shook it gently again. Out popped a blue and white marble!

"Brussels sprouts!" Alex cried. She held up the marble.

"So that was the problem!" exclaimed Janie.

Mother changed the bag on the vacuum and Father turned it on. It ran perfectly, picking up the rest of the popcorn T-Bone had spilled.

Everyone was relieved. Janie took a quick shower to get the dust out of her hair and off her face.

"I think we'll just close up the pantry for the night," Mother decided. "We'll clean it tomorrow."

Mother and Father said another good night to the girls and carried the vacuum up the stairs with them. They hadn't been upstairs a minute before Alex heard them cry, "OH, NO!"

Racing up the stairs to see what was

the matter, the girls joined Mother and Father in front of the pantry and utility closet. After looking inside, they began to giggle.

Although they had forgotten T-Bone, the dog had not forgotten the dog biscuits on the floor of the closet. He had nosed his way through the soap, paper plates, and toothpicks to find and eat each biscuit. He ate the last biscuit in one gulp and then sat down in the middle of the closet looking very pleased with himself.

"Look at his stomach!" Alex cried. "It bulges!"

Everyone laughed.

"T-Bone! You ate almost an entire box of dog biscuits!" Mother scolded the dog.

"Woof!" T-Bone answered. He held out a paw for Mother to shake.

"I think I know one dog who's spending the night outside in his doghouse," declared Father.

"Oh, no! Please let him stay with us!" cried the girls.

"Okay," Father relented, "but he needs to go out for a bit now." He opened the kitchen door and put T-Bone outside.

Mother and Father closed up the pantry and went back upstairs. The girls went downstairs to watch the rest of the movie. When the movie was over, they let T-Bone back inside and stayed awake for a while longer. The last thing Alex thought of as she drifted off to sleep was the vacuum cleaner and the bag of dust that had exploded in Janie's face. She could not help but giggle herself to sleep.

At school the next week, Alex's class was busy getting ready for the sixth-grade graduation ceremonies to be held the following week. On the last day of school, the sixth graders and their parents would attend a breakfast where the children would receive their diplomas.

Mrs. Shivers brought the class to the gymnasium where they could rehearse a special song they planned to sing for their parents at the graduation breakfast. Mrs. Shivers wanted to rehearse on the stage. She positioned the children in three rows on the stage. Alex stood in the center of the first row in front of the microphone. She had the job of introducing the song to the parents.

As Alex took her place on stage, she was surprised to hear thunder crash outside. It was quite unusual to hear a storm from inside the gymnasium. Mrs. Shivers paused in her instructions as the lights in the room flickered briefly.

"We must be having quite a thunderstorm outside," Mrs. Shivers told the class.

Alex forgot all about the storm as she stepped up to the microphone to rehearse her introduction. She had just finished speaking and returned to her place in the front row of children when a gigantic thunderclap sounded, and was followed by a loud POP! The lights in the room flickered and went out, plunging the gymnasium into total darkness.

"AHHHHHH!" everyone cried at once.

"Oh, dear!" Mrs. Shivers exclaimed.

"HELP!" some children called out.

"Hey, where's the lights?" others shouted.

Several children in the back row began to push their way forward. Alex felt the group behind her begin to press up against her.

"Hey! Stop pushing!" Alex shouted. "You're gonna push me off the stage!"

"CHILDREN!" Mrs. Shivers clapped her hands to get their attention. "Everybody stand still! Don't push!"

But the mob of children continued to push forward. Alex tried to push backward. She bumped into the microphone stand as the children kept pushing. Suddenly, there was a tremendous crash as the microphone stand fell off the stage to the floor below.

The loud noise stopped the forward movement of the mob. A stunned silence filled the room.

"CHILDREN!" Mrs. Shivers shouted in a commanding voice. "I want everyone to sit down right where you are. Do not move another inch forward!"

This time the children obeyed their teacher. With a few bumps and scuffles, everyone sat down in the darkness.

Alex breathed a sigh of relief. The edge of the stage was only a few inches away. She could very easily have been pushed over the edge like the microphone stand.

"Thank You, Lord Jesus," Alex whispered in the darkness. She had no doubt that God had saved her.

"Just sit still," Mrs. Shivers told the children. "I'm sure the electricity will come back on in a minute."

But the electricity did not come back on, and it was dark! It was so dark that Alex could not see her hand when she held it up in front of her face. It was both scary and exciting to sit on the stage in the gymnasium in complete blackness. If Alex hadn't been sitting right on the edge of the stage, she would have felt better.

After a few minutes, Mrs. Shivers found her way to the door that led to the hallway. She opened it and a faint light shone in from the hall, but it was not enough for the children to make their way safely off the stage.

"CAN ANYBODY HEAR ME?" Mrs. Shivers stood in the doorway and called out. "WE NEED HELP! HELP!"

The teacher continued to call for help until finally Mr. Whitney, the school custodian, answered her call.

"HANG ON!" Mr. Whitney shouted. "I'M COMING!"

Before long, a beam of light appeared in the doorway. Mr. Whitney carried a large flashlight. "I think some power lines blew outside," he said. "Are you all right?"

Mrs. Shivers quickly told Mr. Whitney about the children on the stage. Mr. Whitney hurried over to the stage, and with the aid of his flashlight the children were able to make their way down the steps from the stage. Alex was one of the first to make it off the stage. She walked down the steps with no problem.

Safely on the ground, Alex watched as the other children slowly moved across the stage and down the steps. As she watched each of her friends, she suddenly thought of Rachel. Rachel wouldn't know what was going on! Alex anxiously looked for Rachel as she realized that Rachel couldn't have heard Mrs. Shivers's instructions and wouldn't be able to read her lips in the dark. Rachel was sitting in the darkness without being able to see or hear. Alex shuddered. That would really be scary!

By now most of the children were off the stage, and Rachel was not among them. Mrs. Shivers was counting the children as they came down the steps.

"That's twenty-six," she told Mr. Whitney. "There should be one more."

"And I know who it is," Alex interrupted. "It's Rachel!"

"Oh, my goodness!" Mrs. Shivers exclaimed. "I hope Rachel is all right up there in the dark."

Mr. Whitney shone his flashlight back and forth across the stage. They finally located Rachel. She had scooted toward the back of the stage and was off to one side. Rachel sat with her head down and her arms wrapped around her legs. When the beam of light hit her, she raised her head.

"Come on, little girl," Mr. Whitney called to Rachel. "It's your turn to come down the steps."

"She can't hear you," Alex told the custodian. "Let me go up and get her." Alex turned to Mrs. Shivers, "She'll come down the steps with me."

"Okay, Alex," Mrs. Shivers replied, "but be careful."

Alex climbed back up on the dark stage and walked slowly over to Rachel. Mr. Whitney did his best to light her steps with the flashlight.

"Rachel, come with me down the steps," Alex said. She got as close to Rachel as she could and hoped that Rachel could read her lips in the flashlight's glow.

Rachel did not answer. She stared at

Alex as if she had not understood. Alex could see that she was frightened.

"It's okay," Alex said. She took one of Rachel's hands. "Come with me."

Rachel hesitated and then slowly nodded her head. Alex led Rachel across the stage and down the steps. When Rachel reached the bottom, everyone cheered.

"Thank you, Alex," Mrs. Shivers hugged Alex and Rachel. The other children moved to huddle around them. They all felt better now that everyone was safely off the stage.

Mr. Whitney asked everyone to hold hands and form a line. With Mr. Whitney and his flashlight in the lead, the line of children wove across the gymnasium floor, out the doorway, and up the hallway to the front of the school. The children had a grand time singing, "Heigh Ho! Heigh Ho! It's off to work we go!" Mrs. Shivers even sang along with them.

They held hands and marched all the way back to the classroom. The scary experience had made them feel close to one another.

When the storm was over, the children all got to go home early because the school still had no electricity. Alex said good-bye to Rachel and walked home with Janie, Julie, and Lorraine. The girls chattered about their adventure. They hoped that the electricity would not be restored overnight so that they would not have to go to school the next day.

CHAPTER 9

Go for It

Although it seemed to take forever, the last week of school finally arrived. A special day called Field Day had been set for outside activities. Alex always looked forward to Field Day. But this year would be extra special. The sixth graders had challenged the fifth graders to a game of softball.

The sixth-grade class had picked its team, and Alex was chosen as starting pitcher. Rachel was the catcher. Eddie was to play first base. Julie and Lorraine had been picked as outfielders. Janie had not made the team, but she did not care. She had formed a cheerleading squad and created special cheers just for the occasion.

Field Day dawned bright and sunny—perfect weather for a ball game. Alex hurried to school, carrying her softball mitt and bat. She and her classmates impatiently waited through the morning announcements. Finally the activities began.

Alex participated in all the morning games, winning first place in the one hundred yard dash. She came in second in the long jump, just barely missing first place by half an inch. She and Rachel won first place in the three-legged race, but came in third in the water balloon toss. The balloon had slid through Alex's hands and broken at her feet, spraying cold water all over her legs. Alex fell flat in the gunnysack race, but her relay team came in first to end the morning games. All in all, Alex had done very well. She collected three blue ribbons, one red ribbon, and one white ribbon.

At lunchtime, Janie ran from table to

table busily teaching the sixth graders her special cheer. They were to shout it loudly as they marched down to the softball diamond right after lunch.

Just before the game, the class lined up on the blacktop. At Janie's signal, they all began to shout the cheer over and over as they made their way to the ball diamond:

SIXTH GRADERS ARE TOUGH TO BEAT,

WE EAT HOT PEPPERS AND RAW MEAT!

Children and teachers alike laughed when they heard the sixth-grade cheer. Mrs. Shivers shook her head and rolled her eyes toward the sky.

From the beginning, the ball game was a complete success for Alex and her classmates. Because they were the home team, the sixth graders were in the field first. They were able to put the fifth-grade batters out one, two, three.

When the sixth grade came to bat,

Alex was the first batter. She led off with a double by smashing one over the shortstop's head and into left field. Then one of the boys hit a choppy single, moving Alex to third base. A third boy struck out. Eddie, the cleanup batter, hit a high one to center field, but the outfielder caught it.

Now there were two outs. It was Rachel's turn to bat. Alex hoped Rachel would not make the third out.

Rachel stepped up to the plate eagerly. Alex thought she looked especially confident. Then Rachel did the very thing Alex had been hoping she would do.

On the very first pitch, Rachel let loose and smacked the ball as hard as she could. The ball soared over the center fielder's head and over the fence at the back of the school property. It bounced into a neighbor's backyard. This time, however, it did not break a window.

Alex skipped across home plate, then turned and watched happily as the other runner, followed by Rachel, came home. The score was 3-0 for the sixth-grade team.

After congratulating Rachel, Alex enjoyed listening to the boys' comments.

"I can't believe it!" Eddie said over and over. He fell to the ground in a pretend faint.

The sixth graders went on to win the ball game with a score of 14-2. The fifth grade did not seem able to do anything right. Alex hit a home run herself in the bottom of the third inning, bringing in two runs. All in all, it was a tremendous victory for the sixth-grade team. Alex and Rachel walked away happily. They hoped it would be the first of many wins that they would have on the ball field. They looked forward to playing summer ball games together.

The very last day of school proved to be quite exciting for Alex. When she awoke, she discovered a large package sitting on the table beside her bed. It was wrapped in paper that had graduation caps all over it.

Rubbing the sleep out of her eyes, Alex opened the card attached to the package. It said, "Happy Graduation," and was signed by her parents.

Alex hurriedly ripped open the package. What she found made her laugh out loud. It was a large, stuffed crocodile! On its back was a place for people to sign their autographs.

"We thought you might want to get all your sixth-grade friends to sign the crocodile," said Mother, appearing suddenly in Alex's doorway.

"That way when you're the Great Crocodile Meatloaf Missionary, you can look at your stuffed crocodile and remember the sixth grade and how you first learned about God's mission for your life," explained Father with a wink.

"Thank you!" cried Alex, running to

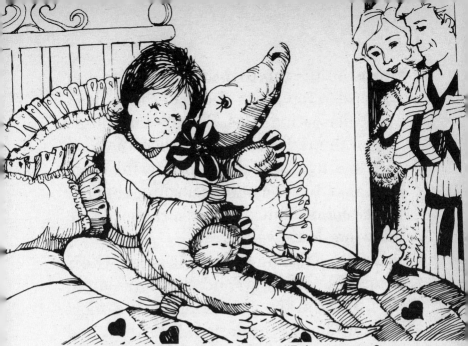

give her parents a hug. "It's a perfect graduation gift."

Alex hurried to get dressed. This was a special day. It was her last day as a student at Kingswood Elementary School. This morning she and her parents were attending the sixth-grade graduation breakfast.

When Alex and her parents arrived at school, they found long tables set up in the gymnasium. The tables were covered with white paper tablecloths. Vases of flowers decorated them. Alex and her parents found seats at one of the tables.

Before eating, Mrs. Shivers introduced the sixth-grade class and called them up to the stage to sing their special song. Alex was a little nervous about giving her introduction, but she had practiced and knew her lines well.

After the class had finished their song and all returned to their seats, Mrs. Larson, the principal, made a short speech about graduation. She then had a special announcement.

"As you know, every year the teachers at Kingswood Elementary School give an award to a sixth-grade student whom they feel is an outstanding achiever. Their selection is based not only on grades, but also on personality, motivation, help-fulness, and an overall good attitude. The award is given to someone whom the teachers believe will be highly successful in life," Mrs. Larson paused and then nodded directly at Alex. "This year's outstanding student award goes to Alexandria Brackenbury!"

Alex felt her face flush. She drew in a sharp breath of air. Her mother hugged her and her father clapped her on the back. Her friends cheered. Alex slowly rose from her seat and walked to the stage where Mrs. Larson was waiting.

Mrs. Larson congratulated Alex and gave her a gold plaque. Alex's name was engraved on the plaque under the words, "Kingswood Elementary School Outstanding Student Award." Alex said an embarrassed "Thank you" into the microphone and hurried off the stage.

On her walk back to her seat, Alex looked at the table full of teachers in the back of the room. There were all of the teachers who had taught her through the years. There was the Bulldozer, Alex's second-grade teacher, whose real name was Mrs. Peppercorn. The Bulldozer had struck fear into Alex's heart until she finally realized that the stern teacher cared deeply for her students. There was Mrs. Tuttle and Mrs. Hibbits. There was also Mr. Carpenter, who had taught Alex and Lorraine how to run a mile properly. Alex felt a twinge of sadness at the thought of leaving them. Her teachers had really become her friends.

Back at her table, Alex was surrounded by friends. "I knew you would get the award!" Janie declared. "It just had to go to you."

"I thought so, too," added Rachel. "You are an extra-special person."

Alex blushed. She was too overwhelmed to answer. She watched as her friends ran to get in the food line where there was an assortment of fruit, donuts, and sweet rolls.

Father put his arm around Alex. "You have done very well, Firecracker, to win this award." He touched the gold plaque.

"Yes, I'd say you are a winner all the way around, honey," added Mother. "All your effort in helping Rachel has paid off. Look at her face. Have you ever seen anyone so happy?"

Alex looked over at her new friend. Rachel stood in the food line, her face radiating joy as she talked to several friends.

"I'd say your latest mission has been quite a success," Father winked at Alex. "What does the Great Crocodile Meatloaf Missionary plan to do next?"

"Eat!" Alex answered immediately. "This whole thing has made me hungry!" She ran to join Rachel and Janie in the food line. She could hear her father's booming laugh echo around the room.

After the breakfast was over, Alex rushed to the teachers' table to have them sign her crocodile. When she explained the meaning behind it, they all laughed.

Alex spent the rest of the day cleaning out her desk and saying good-bye to old friends. It did not matter that everyone would attend the same middle school next year. Leaving grade school marked the end of an important period in their lives.

Janie said it best when she remarked, "It's like we're no longer children. We're kinda halfway between children and adults. I mean, just think, next year we'll be teenagers!"

"Yeah, I know," Alex replied. "It's really exciting and scary at the same time."

Alex and Janie walked out of the school building and looked back at Kingswood Elementary for the last time.

"I guess everybody grows up," Janie said a little sadly.

Alex nodded. She looked down at the stuffed crocodile she carried in her arms. "Brussels sprouts, Janie, let's not be sad," she told her best friend. "We're starting out on a new adventure, and God's got a special mission for your life and for mine. Let's go for it!"

With that, Alex and Janie marched out of the school yard to climb the Juniper Street hill one last time.

Amen